Click Start
A Select-Your-Story Adventure

SCRIPT BY **Joe Caramagna** LAYOUT BY **Emilio Urbano**

CLEAN UP AND INKS BY **Andrea Greppi, Marco Forcelloni, Michela Frare**

COLORING BY **Angela Capolupo, Giuseppe Fontana, Massimo Rocca**

LETTERING BY **Chris Dickey**

Heart from the Start, Eyes on the Prize

SCRIPT AND PENCILS BY **Amy Mebberson**

CLEAN UP AND INKS BY **Michela Frare** COLORING BY **Dan Jackson**

LETTERING BY **Richard Starkings** AND **Comicraft's Jimmy Betancourt**

COVER ART BY
Emilio Urbano, Andrea Greppi, Angela Capolupo

Dark Horse Books

DARK HORSE BOOKS

president and publisher **Mike Richardson**

collection editor **Freddye Miller**

collection assistant editor **Judy Khuu**

designer **David Nestelle, Chris Dickey**

digital art technician **Samantha Hummer**

Neil Hankerson Executive Vice President • Tom Weddle Chief Financial Officer • Randy Stradley Vice President of Publishing • Nick McWhorter Chief Business Development Officer • Dale LaFountain Chief Information Officer • Matt Parkinson Vice President of Marketing • Cara Niece Vice President of Production and Scheduling • Mark Bernardi Vice President of Book Trade and Digital Sales • Ken Lizzi General Counsel • Dave Marshall Editor in Chief • Davey Estrada Editorial Director • Chris Warner Senior Books Editor • Cary Grazzini Director of Specialty Projects • Lia Ribacchi Art Director • Vanessa Todd-Holmes Director of Print Purchasing • Matt Dryer Director of Digital Art and Prepress • Michael Gombos Director of International Publishing and Licensing • Kari Yadro Director of Custom Programs • Kari Torson Director of International Licensing

DISNEY PUBLISHING WORLDWIDE GLOBAL MAGAZINES, COMICS AND PARTWORKS
PUBLISHER Lynn Waggoner • EDITORIAL TEAM Bianca Coletti (Director, Magazines), Guido Frazzini (Director, Comics), Carlotta Quattrocolo (Executive Editor), Stefano Ambrosio (Executive Editor, New IP), Camilla Vedove (Senior Manager, Editorial Development), Behnoosh Khalili (Senior Editor), Julie Dorris (Senior Editor—Click Start Project Lead), Mina Riazi (Assistant Editor), Jonathan Manning (Assistant Editor) • DESIGN Enrico Soave (Senior Designer) • ART Ken Shue (VP, Global Art), Manny Mederos (Senior Illustration Manager, Comics and Magazines), Roberto Santillo (Creative Director), Marco Ghiglione (Creative Manager), Stefano Attardi (Computer Art Designer) • PORTFOLIO MANAGEMENT Olivia Ciancarelli (Director) • BUSINESS & MARKETING Mariantonietta Galla (Marketing Manager), Virpi Korhonen (Editorial Manager)

SPECIAL THANKS to Rich Moore, Phil Johnston, Clark Spencer, Jim Reardon, Cory Loftis, Matthias Lechner, Ami Thompson, Stevi Carter, Brittany Kikuchi, Simona Grandi, Jeff Clark, Alison Giordano, and Luca Pisanu.

Ralph Breaks the Internet: Click Start—A Select-Your-Story Adventure
(Scholastic Edition)

Published by Dark Horse Books
A division of Dark Horse Comics, Inc.
10956 SE Main Street
Milwaukie, OR 97222

DarkHorse.com

To find a comics shop in your area, visit comicshoplocator.com

Scholastic edition: December 2018
ISBN 978-1-50671-325-0

1 3 5 7 9 10 8 6 4 2
Printed in Canada

Meet the Players!

Wreck-It Ralph

The Bad Guy from the 8-bit video game, *Fix-It Felix, Jr.* Ralph's job is to wreck all things in Niceland. But Ralph is much more than the role he plays, and he's not a *bad* guy. He is very talented at wrecking things, however, and has to be careful to make sure to use his ability to his advantage—and to everyone else's. Not long ago, Ralph found his best friend forever, racer Vanellope von Schweetz.

Vanellope von Schweetz

The best racer in the candy kart racing game, *Sugar Rush.* Vanellope is sharp-witted, spunky, and fun-loving, and she shows no pretension when it comes to being a princess. Vanellope has been setting the track on fire ever since Wreck-It Ralph visited her game and helped her to regain her rightful place as ruler of *Sugar Rush.* And while she loves her race, she longs for something different . . .

Now, let's go to the internet!

Welcome to the internet, friendo!

You're about to enter a fun-filled adventure where *you* choose a path for your favorite video game heroes, Ralph and Vanellope.

To select your own story, all you have to do is follow the instruction icons at the bottom of each page and make your choice!

To begin selecting your story, click START

START
GO TO PAGE 7

To skip to Vanellope's adventure in Oh My Disney, click SKIP

SKIP
GO TO PAGE 55

WHATEVER IT'S CALLED—IF WE **DON'T** GET THE STEERING WHEEL FROM THERE IN THE NEXT THREE HOURS, IT CAN'T BE DELIVERED BEFORE THE SALVAGE GUY COMES TO LITWAK'S TO SELL YOUR GAME FOR PARTS!

YOU'LL BE **HOMELESS!**

CONGRATULATIONS! YOU'RE A WINNER!

WHAT'D YOU WIN?

DON'T GET DISTRACTED

ME?! WHAT'D I WIN?

SEVEN TRICKS TO GET RID OF YOUR BELLY FAT! NUMBER SIX WILL **AMAZE** YOU!

Congratulations You Won!!
WINNER !!!

HEY! THAT'S NOT **NICE**—

DON'T GET **DISTRACTED,** RALPH! WE'RE ON THE CLOCK—

SWEET LORDY BGORDY! LOOK AT ALL THOSE **RACING** GAMES!

HEY, ARE THOSE **FREE COOKIES** OVER THERE?

TIRED OF BEING **BALD?**

COMPUTER RUNNING SLOWLY?

WARNING! THIS SITE USES **COOKIES!**

THIS PLACE SURE IS DISTRACTING.

EYES ON THE **PRIZE,** CHUMBO! EBAY, REMEMBER?

OH, HEY! LOOK! MAYBE THAT LITTLE **EGG GUY** CAN TELL US HOW TO **GET** THERE.

TO FOLLOW VANELLOPE, GO TO PAGE 14!

TO FOLLOW BOTH, GO TO PAGE 22!

TO FOLLOW RALPH, GO TO PAGE 18!

TO CHECK IN WITH FELIX, TURN THE PAGE!

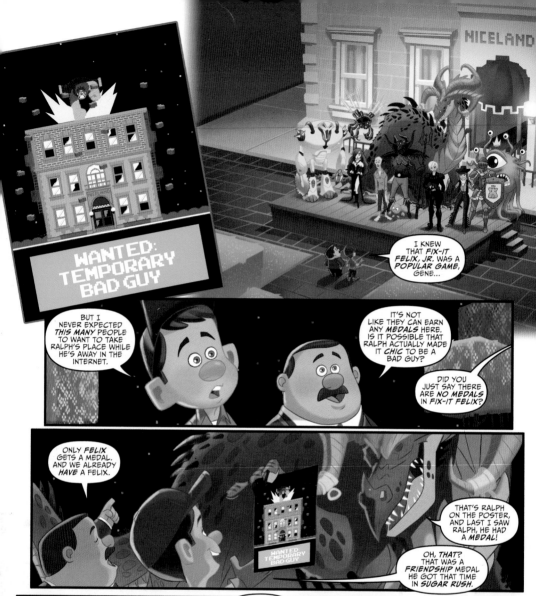

WANTED: TEMPORARY BAD GUY

I KNEW THAT *FIX-IT FELIX, JR.* WAS A *POPULAR GAME*, GENE...

BUT I NEVER EXPECTED *THIS MANY* PEOPLE TO WANT TO TAKE RALPH'S PLACE WHILE HE'S AWAY IN THE INTERNET.

IT'S NOT LIKE THEY CAN EARN ANY *MEDALS* HERE. IS IT POSSIBLE THAT RALPH ACTUALLY MADE IT *CHIC* TO BE A BAD GUY?

DID YOU JUST SAY THERE ARE *NO MEDALS* IN *FIX-IT FELIX?*

ONLY *FELIX* GETS A MEDAL. AND WE ALREADY *HAVE* A FELIX.

WANTED TEMPORARY BAD GUY

THAT'S RALPH ON THE POSTER, AND LAST I SAW RALPH, HE HAD A *MEDAL!*

OH, *THAT?* THAT WAS A *FRIENDSHIP* MEDAL HE GOT THAT TIME IN *SUGAR RUSH.*

Y'ALL HEAR THAT? THEY'RE GIVING OUT MEDALS OVER AT *SUGAR RUSH!* LET'S GO!

NO, WAIT!

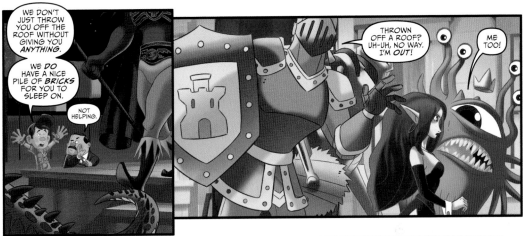

WE DON'T JUST THROW YOU OFF THE ROOF WITHOUT GIVING YOU *ANYTHING.*

WE *DO* HAVE A NICE PILE OF *BRICKS* FOR YOU TO SLEEP ON.

NOT HELPING.

THROWN OFF A ROOF? UH-UH, NO WAY. I'M *OUT!*

ME TOO!

WHAT— A *CY-BUG!*

WELL...

AT LEAST THERE ARE STILL *FOUR* OF YOU WE CAN AUDITION—

GET WRECKED, YOU GLORIFIED CAN OPENER!

KRSSH!

THREE. THREE OF YOU.

ISN'T CALHOUN JUST THE *TOPS?*

WE HAVE TO BE *OBJECTIVE* HERE, FELIX— EVEN THOUGH SHE'S YOUR *WIFE.*

TO AUDITION ZOMBIE, GO TO PAGE 24!

TO AUDITION SOUR BILL, GO TO PAGE 30!

TO AUDITION CALHOUN, GO TO PAGE 38!

SWEET SOURDOUGH!

WHAT'S THE *BIG IDEA* HERE?

IT'S A *SLOWDOWN.* THERE'S HEAVY *TRAFFIC* UP AHEAD, THAT'S ALL.

NOT SURE WHEN IT'LL LIGHTEN UP, BUT YOU CAN TRY AND *REFRESH* IN THE MEANTIME.

OKAY, THEN, *REFRESH* ME!

I'LL TAKE A *ROOT BEER FLOAT,* PLEASE! WITH STRAWBERRY ICE CREAM, WHIPPED CREAM, AND—OOH!—A BIG RED CHERRY ON TOP!

I—WHAT?! NO. I DON'T MEAN *THAT* KIND OF REFRESHMENT.

IS YOUR INTERNET *TOO* SLOW?

I MEANT START AGAIN IN A NEW *POD.*

OHHH, I SEE—

TO REFRESH AS RALPH, GO TO PAGE 19!

TO EXPLORE ON FOOT, TURN THE PAGE!

TO SEARCH THE WAREHOUSE FOR THE STEERING WHEEL, GO TO PAGE 26!

TO ZOOM YOUR POD TO EBAY, GO TO PAGE 50!

THANK YOU, MR. KNOWSMORE!

CLICK!

Redirecting to eBay.

WHOA! *SWEET RIDE!*

WAIT UP, KID!

WOOOOOOOOO!

WHOA.

DO YOU WISH TO MAKE A QUERY?

NO, NO, NOT *ME.* I'VE HAD ENOUGH *HIGH SPEED* FOR ONE DAY— VANELLOPE'S THE *RACER.* THESE BIG FEET WERE MADE FOR WALKING.

I'D ADVISE AGAINST THAT. THE INTERNET IS FILLED WITH *DISTRACTIONS.*

FOR SOME, MAYBE, BUT I'VE GOT *LASER-LIKE* FOCUS—

OOOOOH! COOKIES!

MOMENTS LATER...

I'VE GOT TO FIND MORE OF THOSE *FREE COOKIE* POP-UPS—

NO, RALPH— WE'VE GOT TO FIND *VANELLOPE* FIRST! LASER FOCUS, LASER FOCUS...

DON'T COME ANY CLOSER! THIS SITE IS *UNSTABLE!*

HM. SEEMS PERFECTLY SAFE TO ME.

HARDLY! IT'S FILLED WITH BAD *COOKIES!*

COOKIES?! YOU DON'T SAY!

I MEAN, YOU DON'T SAY...

SURE, TRACKING COOKIES *SEEMS* HARMLESS, BUT YOU'LL HAVE TO *LOG OFF* TO GET RID OF THEM...

'CAUSE ONCE THEY'RE IN YOUR SYSTEM, THEY'RE *SO HARD* TO GET RID OF.

TELL ME ABOUT IT. IT'S *TERRIBLE.*

NO— IT'S DOWNRIGHT *OFFENSIVE* IS WHAT IT IS!

YOU KNOW WHAT I'M GONNA DO?

I'M GONNA MARCH RIGHT IN THERE AND GIVE THAT MAL A *WHAT FOR* AND *PIECE OF MY MIND* AND *ALL O' THAT!*

WAIT—

YOU'RE DOING A GREAT PUBLIC SERVICE! *THANK YOU!*

CREEEAK

AHOY! I BE **MALLORY**, THE **PROPRIETOR** OF THIS HERE ESTABLISHMENT— THE LARGEST COLLECTION OF **BOOTLEG MOVIES** IN THE INTERNET!

SWEET MAMMA JAMMA! IT'S THE COOKIE **MOTHER LODE.**

AND WHAT BE YER **NAME?**

RALPH. WRECK-IT RALPH.

AND WHAT'S YER SECRET **PASSWORD,** RALPH-WRECK-IT-RALPH?

PASSWORD? UH...LET'S SEE...

UP, DOWN... LEFT, RIGHT... ...A, B... START?

ARGH! YER BREATH BE PUNGENT ENOUGH TO SEND A GAL TO DAVY JONES' LOCKER!

SO... WE'RE **GOOD?** ARE THESE COOKIES FOR, LIKE, EVERYONE, OR...

INDULGE YERSELF, MATEY.

HOW ABOUT **YOU?** WHAT'S YER PREFERENCE?

!

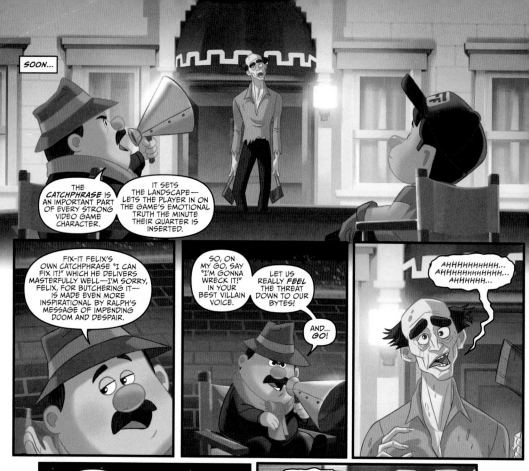

SOON...

THE *CATCHPHRASE* IS AN IMPORTANT PART OF EVERY STRONG VIDEO GAME CHARACTER.

IT SETS THE LANDSCAPE— LETS THE PLAYER IN ON THE GAME'S EMOTIONAL TRUTH THE MINUTE THEIR QUARTER IS INSERTED.

FIX-IT FELIX'S OWN CATCHPHRASE "I CAN FIX IT!" WHICH HE DELIVERS MASTERFULLY WELL—I'M SORRY, FELIX, FOR BUTCHERING IT— IS MADE EVEN MORE INSPIRATIONAL BY RALPH'S MESSAGE OF IMPENDING DOOM AND DESPAIR.

SO, ON MY GO, SAY "I'M GONNA WRECK IT!" IN YOUR BEST VILLAIN VOICE.

LET US REALLY *FEEL* THE THREAT DOWN TO OUR BYTES!

AND... GO!

AHHHHHHHHH... AHHHHHHHHHHHH... AHHHHH...

NO, NO. AGAIN, WITH *GUSTO.* "I'M GONNA WRECK IT!"

AHHHHHHHHHH... AHHHHHHHHHHHH...

OOOKAY, WELL—

AHHHHHHHHHH...

GIVE HIM A MINUTE. ZOMBIES *APPEAR* TO MOVE SLOWLY, BUT TURN YOUR HEAD AND— *BINGO!*—THEY'RE ON YOU LIKE ANTS ON A PEANUT BUTTER AND JELLY SANDWICH.

COME ON. "I'M GONNA WRECK IT."

AHHHHHH'M GONNAAAAA AHHHHHHH...

"WRECK IT."

...AHHHHH... AHHHHHH...

OPEN YOUR MOUTH NICE AND WIDE. USE YOUR DIAPHRAGM. LIKE THIS—

I'M GONNA WRECK IT!

AAHHHHHH... AHHH'M...GONNA WRECK IT!

KRAKK

S-SEE, GENE? I *TOLD* YOU.

I CAN'T BELIEVE I'M SAYING THIS...

BUT I THINK I MISS RALPH.

TO AUDITION SOUR BILL, GO TO PAGE 30!

TO AUDITION CALHOUN, GO TO PAGE 38!

TO DECIDE RALPH CAN'T BE REPLACED, GO TO PAGE 48!

LET'S SEE... LOUNGE CHAIRS, OFFICE CHAIRS, BAR STOOLS— AH!

BEACH CHAIRS!

THIS CART WILL TAKE YOU TO OUR *LEISURE* SECTION AND OUR *BEST SELLERS* WILL BE ON YOUR RIGHT.

‡GASP!‡

HOLY ONION COLA! WHAT HAPPENED?!

HE LOGGED OFF WITHOUT CHECKING OUT. HAPPENS ALL THE TIME.

TO SHOP FOR THE STEERING WHEEL IN THE WAREHOUSE, GO TO PAGE 32!

TO SWITCH TO RALPH, GO TO PAGE 42!

AAAAAAAAH!

KRASSH!

YEEEARAHH! Maj's CLICK! Warehouse

FREE COOKIES

WOO-HOO!

IS—IS THAT WHAT I *THINK* THAT IS?

NO, IT *CAN'T* BE—

IT *IS*! IT'S A *SUGAR RUSH* STEERING WHEEL!

BUT THAT'S NOT EBAY—IT'S A PLACE CALLED IN... STA...GERR...AM! *INSTAGRAM!*

#SaveSugarRush

TH-THAT *BIRD*...WHERE DID IT COME FROM?

TO SEARCH INSTAGRAM, GO TO PAGE 34!

TO FOLLOW THE BIRD, GO TO PAGE 42!

TO SWITCH TO VANELLOPE, GO TO PAGE 32!

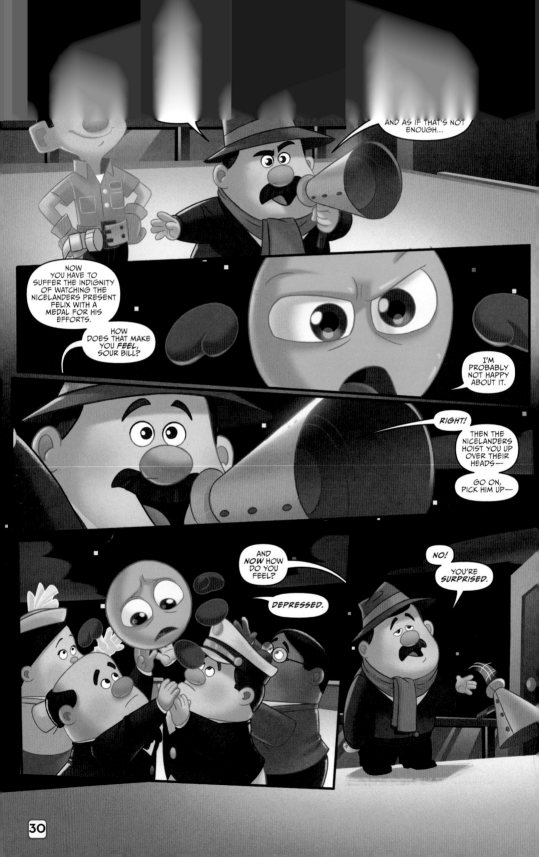

TO RACE, GO TO PAGE 36!

WHOA. WHAT IS THIS PLACE?

WELCOME TO THE INSTAGRAM MUSEUM.

SIR! YOUR FEET!

YUP, THEY SURE ARE. GOT TWO BIG HANDS TOO.

OH, I SEE—THIS IS ONE OF THEM FANCY JOINTS.

BUT, LOOK—THERE'S ANOTHER PAIR OF BARE FEET RIGHT OVER THERE.

AH, YES, THIS IS ONE OF OUR MOST POPULAR EXHIBITS—"BARE FEET BY THE POOL." YOU'LL BE SWIPING THROUGH THOSE FOR DAYS.

IT'S SECOND ONLY TO "BARE FEET ON THE BEACH."

YOU SURE HAVE A LOT OF PICTURES OF CATS AROUND HERE.

IS...IS SOMETHING WRONG?

RUMMMMBBLLL

WHAT'S THAT TIC-TAC-TOE SIGN MEAN?

IT'S CALLED A *HASHTAG*. IS THERE SOMETHING SPECIFIC I CAN HELP YOU FIND... SO YOU AND YOUR BIG BARE FEET CAN BE ON YOUR WAY?

I SAW A STEERING WHEEL FROM *SUGAR RUSH* ON THE SIGN OUTSIDE—

SUGAR RUSH! YES! THAT'S BEEN *TRENDING* TODAY.

HASHTAG FIX SUGAR RUSH?

"*SUGAR RUSH* IS OUT OF ORDER" WITH A SAD FACE.

THERE ARE SO MANY OF THESE! ALL OF THESE PEOPLE ARE *COUNTING* ON US. WE'VE GOT TO FIND EBAY AND GET THAT *STEERING WHEEL!*

PARDON? WHO'S "WE"?

RUMMMBOBILLE

UNFF. SOMETHING'S NOT SITTIN' RIGHT.

DON'T GET SICK IN *HERE!* NET-E.R.'S RIGHT ACROSS THE STREET...

I'VE GOTTA GET *OUT OF* HERE!

GO TO PAGE 50!

Help Vanellope navigate the warehouse. If you choose your twists and turns wisely, she might be the first to the finish line!

YOU WON THE RACE TO THE FLASH SALE! GO TO PAGE 46!

YOU LOST! GO TO PAGE 40!

SERGEANT CALHOUN, I UNDERSTAND YOU FANCY YOURSELF AN EXPERT IN MASS DESTRUCTION.

I TAKE PRIDE IN POUNDING *CY-BUGS* INTO *SCRAP METAL*, BUT I'LL PRETTY MUCH DESTROY ANYONE OR ANYTHING WHO STANDS IN THE WAY OF WHAT I WANT.

ISN'T MY WIFE A *DYNAMITE GAL?* IF ANYONE CAN REPLACE RALPH IT'S HER.

FELIX, PLEASE— *OBJECTIVITY,* REMEMBER?

SERGEANT, THEY CALL HIM WRECK-IT RALPH FOR A *REASON.* HIS JOB IS TO WRECK THE NICELAND APARTMENT BUILDING SO FELIX CAN FIX IT WITH HIS MAGIC HAMMER AND GET HIS MEDAL.

OBSERVE WHILE I DEMONSTRATE ON THE MODEL, THEN IT'S *YOUR* TURN.

THIS OUGHTTA BE GOOD.

I'M GONNA WRECK IT!

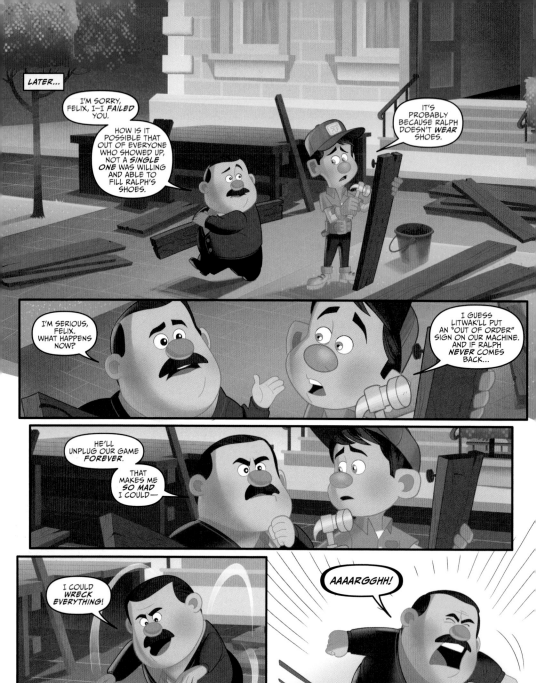

LATER...

I'M SORRY, FELIX, I—I *FAILED* YOU.

HOW IS IT POSSIBLE THAT OUT OF EVERYONE WHO SHOWED UP, NOT A *SINGLE ONE* WAS WILLING AND ABLE TO FILL RALPH'S SHOES.

IT'S PROBABLY BECAUSE RALPH DOESN'T *WEAR* SHOES.

I'M SERIOUS, FELIX. WHAT HAPPENS NOW?

I GUESS LITWAK'LL PUT AN "OUT OF ORDER" SIGN ON OUR MACHINE. AND IF RALPH *NEVER* COMES BACK...

HE'LL UNPLUG OUR GAME *FOREVER*.

THAT MAKES ME *SO MAD* I COULD—

I COULD *WRECK* EVERYTHING!

SKRAKK!

AAAARGGHH!

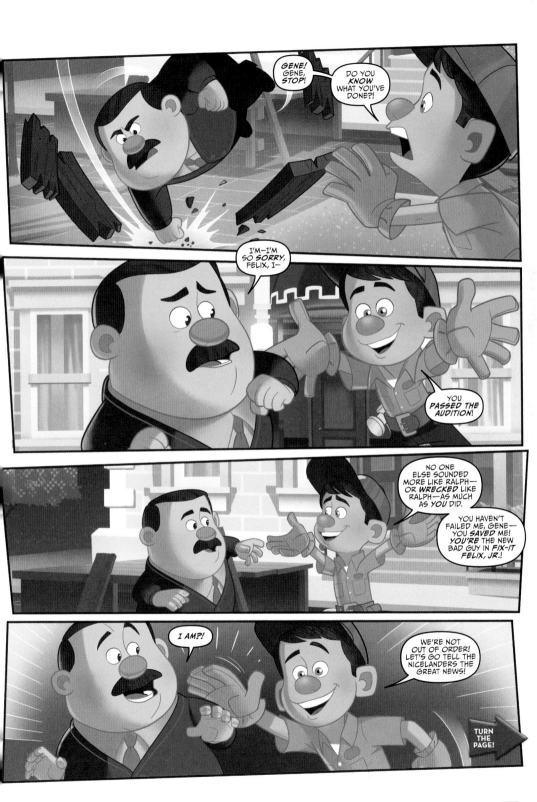

A SHORT WHILE LATER...

VANELLOPE!

STINKBRAIN?!

WHERE HAVE YOU *BEEN*?

IT'S A *LONG* STORY.

WHY AREN'T YOU ALREADY AT EBAY?

IT'S A *LONG* STORY.

5:50

COME ON, RALPHIE BOY, WE'RE RUNNING OUT OF TIME!

KNOWSMO

I'VE BEEN KICKED OFF THE INTERNET.

WHAT DID YOU DO?

RALPH, IT'S WORKING!

LOGGING OFF AGAIN?

ALL OF THESE DANG POP-UP ADS AND THEIR COOKIES— I'VE GOTTA RESTART THE BROWSER!

Internet connection lost!

I'VE GOT THIS ONE OVER HERE—

Heart from the Start, Eyes on the Prize

INSIDE THE *OH MY DISNEY* WEBSITE, THE INTERNET.

AH, SYSTEM MAINTENANCE DAY! TWELVE HOURS OF SWEET, SWEET INTERNET LOAFING!

COAST IS CLEAR, TIME TO CHECK IN ON THE PRINCESSES!

PRINCESSES
THIS IS A RESTRICTED AREA

PRINCESSES
THIS IS A RESTRICTED AREA

FZZT!

HEY HEY! HOW'S THE QUIZZING TODAY, LADIES?

FZZT!

AH! YOU REALLY NEED TO *KNOCK* BEFORE YOU DO THAT!

WE'RE JUST ON LUNCH BREAK, COME ON IN.

OH DEAR...

THE "SNOW" SISTERS NOT HERE?

OH, THEY HAD A SPECIAL ARTICLE THEY HAD TO ATTEND. SOMETHING ABOUT A *STAGE* SHOW!

CAN I HAVE ANNA'S LUNCH IF SHE'S NOT BACK IN FIVE MINUTES?

ARIEL, WHAT DID WE AGREE ABOUT YOUR "COLLECTING"?

≶SIGH≷ "NOTHING PERISHABLE..."

NO RACING TODAY, V?

EH, *SLAUGHTER RACE* IS GETTING UPGRADES, SO, I'VE GOT SOME TIME TO KILL.

YESSS INVITED ME TO BRUNCH AT EPICURIOUS, BUT I FIGURED I'D COME HANG OUT HERE. COMPANY IS BETTER *AND* I DON'T HAVE TO WAIT FOR A SEAT!

FLOP

NOT TO MENTION--PILLOW FIGHTS!

POOF!

ACTUALLY... MAYBE YOU GALS CAN HELP ME WITH SOMETHING.

SO I LOST A COUPLE O' RACES LAST WEEK AND SHANK THINKS I'M COASTING ON MY AWESOME NATURAL TALENT INSTEAD OF TRAINING.

YOU GALS HELPED ME BEFORE. I WAS WONDERING IF YOU HAD ANY UPSKILLING IDEAS ON HOW THE PRINCESS SHINDIG COULD WORK FOR ME AS A *RACER?*

ARIEL, PILLOWS PLUS HOT LIQUID EQUALS *BAD*, REMEMBER...?

WELL, THERE ARE A *LOT* OF WAYS TO BE A PRINCESS, V. ARE YOU READY FOR SO MANY SPECIFICS?

YEAH! HIT ME WITH YOUR BEST LIFE HACKS, GALS!

OH, ME FIRST! I'VE GOT A GOOD ONE, C'MON!

THOSE MACHINES YOU DRIVE HAVE LOTS OF DOOHICKEYS TO MAKE THEM WORK, RIGHT?

SO YOU'RE WHIZZING AROUND AND POOF! A WHOZIBOB *BREAKS.* YOU'RE COMPLETELY STUCK!

WELLLL, *YEAH,* BUT WE JUST WAIT FOR THE GAME TO RESET AN--

VOILÀ! EVERY RACER SHOULD HAVE A GENUINE *DINGLEHOPPER.* A THOUSAND AND ONE USES *AND* EASY TO STOW!

THOK

I HAVE PLENTY!

WHOA, YOU SURE DO!

SPEAKING OF ACCESSORIES, LET'S TALK FIELD OF VISION!

IF YOU'RE GOING TO GO ADVENTURING, YOU NEED TO SEE CLEARLY. THAT MEANS A HEADBAND!

HERE, HAVE ONE OF MY SPARES. IT'S NOT REALLY MY COLOR, ANYWAY...

WELL, OKAY, BUT I CAN'T GUARANTEE THIS WON'T GET STICKY! CANDY HAIR, REMEMBER?

AHA! THERE IT IS, I *KNEW* I HAD A COPY! OVER HERE, V...

...VANELLOPE?

YO.

YOUR "TO BE READ" PILE IS GETTING A LITTLE OUTTA HAND, BELLE.

IT'S A HISTORY OF THE HORSELESS CARRIAGE. A CRAFTSMAN MUST KNOW HER TOOLS! THE CHAPTER ON THE DEVELOPMENT OF THE MULTI-SPEED TRANSMISSION IS JUST *RIVETTING!*

!

ARE THERE PICTURES?

KNOWLEDGE IS POWER. USE IT.

OH, SORRY, YOU'RE NAPPING...

NO I'M NOT. JUST BECAUSE THERE'S QUIET DOESN'T MEAN THERE ARE NO VOICES.

HAVE YOU EVER SAT WITH YOUR CAR AND JUST *LISTENED* TO IT?

Z

WAP!!

WELL, WHEN I'M REVVING AT 5000RPM, IT'S KINDA HARD TO *NOT* HEAR IT!

I'M SAYING LISTEN TO YOUR ENVIRONMENT AND THE SPIRITS AROUND YOU. IT MIGHT BE THAT YOUR CAR IS TELLING YOU MORE THAN YOU THINK.

AND AFTER YOU TAP THAT MAGICAL MOTOR ENERGY, DON'T FORGET THAT *YOU* NEED FUEL TOO!

FINEST TO-GO TREATS FROM THE FINEST RESTAURANT ON THE BAYOU! TO RUN YOUR BUSINESS EFFICIENTLY, YOU NEED NUTRITIOUS, SLOW-BURNING ENERGY!

IF YOU LIKE THEM, PLEASE FEEL FREE TO LEAVE A REVIEW. I'M AIMING FOR THAT THIRD GOLD MICHELIN STAR!

LOOKING FOR BOOKS FOR YOUNGER READERS?

$7.99 each!

EACH VOLUME INCLUDES A SECTION OF FUN ACTIVITIES!

DISNEY·PIXAR INCREDIBLES 2: HEROES AT HOME

Violet and Dash are part of a Super family, and they are trying to help out at home. Can they pick up groceries and secretly stop some bad guys? And then can they clean up the house while Jack-Jack is "sleeping"?

ISBN 978-1-50670-943-7 | $7.99

DISNEY ZOOTOPIA: FRIENDS TO THE RESCUE

Young Judy Hopps proves she's a brave little bunny when she helps a classmate. And can a quick-thinking young Nick Wilde liven up a birthday party? Friends save the day in these tales of Zootopia!

ISBN 978-1-50671-054-9 | $7.99

DISNEY PRINCESS: JASMINE'S NEW PET

Jasmine has a new pet tiger, Rajah, but he's not quite ready for palace life. Will she be able to train the young cub before the Sultan finds him another home?

ISBN 978-1-50671-052-5 | $7.99

For more information or to order direct: On the web: DarkHorse.com | Email: mailorder@darkhorse.com
Phone: 1-800-862-0052 Mon.–Fri. 9 AM to 5 PM Pacific Time

Copyright © 2018 Disney Enterprises, Inc. and Pixar. Dark Horse Books® and the Dark Horse logo are registered trademarks of Dark Horse Comics, Inc. All rights reserved. (BL8019)